SUPERSTARS
of
PRO
FOOTBALL

PLAXICO BURRESS

Robert Grayson

Mason Crest Publishers

Produced by OTTN Publishing in association with
21st Century Publishing and Communications, Inc.

MASON CREST PUBLISHERS INC.
370 Reed Road
Broomall, Pennsylvania 19008
(866) MCP-BOOK (toll free)
www.masoncrest.com

Printed in the United States of America.

First Printing

9 8 7 6 5 4 3 2 1

Library of Congress Cataloging-in-Publication Data

Grayson, Robert, 1951–
    Plaxico Burress / Robert Grayson.
       p. cm. — (Superstars of pro football)
    Includes index.
ISBN 978-1-4222-0552-5 (hardcover) — ISBN 978-1-4222-0821-2 (pbk.)
  1. Burress, Plaxico—Juvenile literature. 2. Football players—United States—
Biography—Juvenile literature. 3. New York Giants (Football team)—Juvenile
literature. I. Title.
GV939.B83G73 2008
796.332092—dc22
[B]   2008024180

Publisher's note:
All quotations in this book come from original sources, and contain the spelling
and grammatical inconsistencies of the original text.

◀◀ CROSS-CURRENTS ▶▶

In the ebb and flow of the currents of life we are each influenced
by many people, places, and events that we directly experience or
have learned about. Throughout the chapters of this book you will
come across **CROSS-CURRENTS** reference bubbles. These bubbles
direct you to a **CROSS-CURRENTS** section in the back of the
book that contains fascinating and informative sidebars
and related pictures. Go on. ▶▶

◀◀CONTENTS▶▶

A
SUPER SEASON

Super Bowl XLII—played on February 3, 2008—was going to be a historic game no matter which team won. For New York Giants wide receiver Plaxico Burress and his teammates, the game would show whether they were championship material or just another team beaten by the New England Patriots on their way to an undefeated 19–0 season.

Playing Hurt

For the Giants to win, Plaxico Burress would have to make his presence known. After all, a few days before the big game Plaxico had predicted that the Giants would defeat the heavily

New York Giants wide receiver Plaxico Burress speaks to reporters during Super Bowl XLII Media Day at the University of Phoenix Stadium in Glendale, Arizona, January 29, 2008.

favored Patriots. Plaxico had some good games for the Giants in the 2007 season, but he was suffering from several injuries going into the Super Bowl. A painful ankle had **hampered** his play since September. A sore knee kept Plaxico from practicing for the championship game. In spite of his injuries, the wide receiver vowed to take the field on Super Bowl Sunday.

Green Bay Packers cornerback Ellis Hobbs, who had trouble covering Plaxico in the NFC Championship game, did not doubt that the wide receiver would have an impact in the big game:

CROSS-CURRENTS

Read "A Brief History of the Super Bowl" to learn more about the biggest game of each NFL season. Go to page 46. ▶▶

> **"**He's got such long arms. A normal throw from Eli [Manning] that is too high for an average receiver is . . . normal for [Burress].**"**

At 6-feet-5-inches and 230 pounds, Plaxico was a big target for Giants **quarterback** Eli Manning. In addition to size, the wide receiver had speed and experience. Manning liked throwing to him. During the regular season, Plaxico was the Giants' leading receiver, with 70 catches for 1,025 yards. He also scored 12 **touchdowns**.

An Uphill Battle

While the Patriots easily made their way into the playoffs, the Giants had a **grueling** season. Unlike the Patriots, who did not lose a game all season, the Giants suffered some tough losses and faced must-win situations throughout the season. There were times when one more loss could have completely wiped out any hope they had of making it to the playoffs.

During the 2007 regular season, the fans and the media had their doubts about whether the Giants could make the playoffs. Some questioned whether Coach Tom Coughlin was right for the team, whether Eli Manning could ever be a top-notch quarterback, and whether Plaxico Burress was playing hard enough and giving 100 percent. As a result of these doubts, the Giants were not considered Super Bowl contenders early in the season. In addition, the Giants had lost to several of the teams they would have to beat in the playoffs to reach the Super Bowl.

A Rocky Season

Despite an up-and-down season in 2007, the Giants had a strength that many people did not notice. Although they didn't have much luck winning in their home stadium, the Giants kept winning on the road. They won so many games on the road that they strung together enough victories to make it to the playoffs.

By the time the regular season ended, the Giants had won seven road games in a row. To get to the Super Bowl, they would first have to win three playoff games on the road. If they lost any of these games, they would be eliminated. Week after week in the playoffs, however, the Giants beat tough opponents. When they

Plaxico Burress drags Philadelphia Eagles cornerback William James down the sidelines after a catch, September 30, 2007. The Giants won the game, 16–3. Plaxico's size and strength—combined with his excellent speed—make him very difficult to cover.

won the NFC Championship game against the Green Bay Packers on January 20, 2008, at Green Bay's Lambeau Field, the Giants had racked up ten straight road wins. They seemed unbeatable away from Giants Stadium.

Plaxico had an incredible game against the Packers. He caught 11 passes for 151 yards. The eight-year veteran of the NFL seemed unstoppable. Once the Giants had beaten the Packers to make it to the Super Bowl, it is no wonder Plaxico firmly believed they could beat the highly favored New England Patriots. Super Bowl XLII was

New England Patriots cornerback Ellis Hobbs isn't close enough to stop Plaxico Burress from pulling down an Eli Manning pass in the end zone with just 35 seconds left in Super Bowl XLII. The touchdown gave New York an improbable 17–14 victory.

to be held at the University of Phoenix Stadium, in Glendale, Arizona. The Giants would again be playing where they were most comfortable—on the road.

A Super Prediction

Five days before the Super Bowl, Plaxico told reporters that the Giants would ruin the Patriots' undefeated season by beating them in the Super Bowl. He **reiterated** that claim a few days later:

> **❝I am going to say it again, the goal is to win the football game. It is not to come here and just play. The goal is to come here and win.❞**

Plaxico's faith in himself and his team was not misplaced. The Super Bowl turned out to be a tough, seesaw battle, and the Giants played their hearts out. The score stayed close for most of the game. The Patriots, however, scored a touchdown with less than three minutes left to play, taking a 14–10 lead. The Patriots were known for holding onto late-game leads. The possibility of a Giants victory seemed to be slipping away.

Refusing to give up, the Giants took the field and fought back. Keeping their hopes alive, the Giants gained ground toward the end zone. The team made several breathtaking plays as they moved the ball. Then, with just 35 seconds left to play, Giants quarterback Eli Manning got the ball and looked downfield to see a welcome sight. Plaxico Burress was heading to the end zone. Manning heaved the football, and Plaxico caught it. With that catch, Plaxico Burress scored the touchdown that nailed down the Giants' 17–14 Super Bowl win.

CROSS-CURRENTS

Read "What Is a Wide Receiver?" to find out more about Plaxico's duties on the football field. Go to page 47. ▶▶

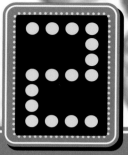

A STAR FROM THE START

As a high school athlete, Plaxico Burress excelled in both basketball and football. Basketball was his first love. He worked hard at the game, and was a star on his high school team. It was in football, however, that professional scouts felt Plaxico could best use his height, strength, and speed.

Plaxico was born on August 12, 1977, in Virginia Beach, Virginia. He and his two brothers, Rick and Carlos, were raised in a single-parent household. His mother, Adelaide Vicki Burress, worked two jobs to support the family. Plaxico remembers that she never complained. In an Associated Press interview, he also credited his grandmother, Louise Elliott, with keeping the family strong. Plaxico recalls,

Plaxico Burress has always been an intense competitor. In high school he starred not just in football, but also in basketball and track. In his senior year, Plaxico was named All-State in basketball, and he was Virginia's state champion in the 300 intermediate hurdles.

"My grandma was sort of a rock . . . . Everyone leaned on her. She was a quiet one who walked with swagger . . . I think my mom got a lot from her."

Plaxico was always interested in sports. Both his mother and his grandmother instilled in him the confidence he needed to be a successful athlete. When he was young, Plaxico learned a lot from watching the older kids in the neighborhood play basketball and football. Eventually, he joined the action. He believed he could be an outstanding player.

A view of Virginia Beach, a city of more than 400,000 residents that is located in eastern Virginia. Plaxico Burress was born and raised in Virginia Beach.

A Top-notch Playmaker

When he entered Green Run High School in Virginia Beach in 1992, Plaxico played on as many sports teams as he could. As a sophomore on the Green Run Stallions football team, Plaxico caught 32 passes, gaining 676 yards, and scored seven touchdowns. He felt he could have done even more if the other teams had not used two or three defenders to guard him. The heavy coverage frustrated him, and he admits that it got in the way of his game. He recalls,

> **My grandmother would actually leave. She'd see me getting disgusted out on the field and get up and leave. She saw what I was doing. I wouldn't try to jump for passes that weren't right to me and I didn't always play hard. I was immature.**

State Champs

Plaxico's play was good enough to lead his team to a state championship. In his junior year, he returned an inch taller and 30 pounds heavier. To help Plaxico learn to deal with the tight defense, his coach, Cadillac Harris, brought in Quincy Bethea to work with him. Bethea had been a top wide receiver with the Stallions' rival, First Colonial High School, and a football star at Appalachian State University. Plaxico learned a great deal from Bethea. He soon continued his assault on opposing schools.

By the time Plaxico's high school football career came to an end, he had helped lead the Stallions to three state championships. He also set school records for a wide receiver with 86 catches and 38 touchdowns. In his senior year, Plaxico was rated the best receiver in the country by *Scholastic Sports*. He also played free safety on the Stallions' defensive team. As a senior, he was named to Virginia's All-State team on both offense and defense, and was a *Parade* magazine, *Prep Football Report*, and *National Recruiting Advisor* All-American.

In addition to football success, Plaxico also made the All-State second team in basketball in his senior year. He averaged 19.6 points and 13.2 rebounds a game. In track, he won the state title in the 300 intermediate hurdles as a senior.

In spite of his athletic achievements, Plaxico had to get his grades up before going to college. To improve his grades, he attended Fork

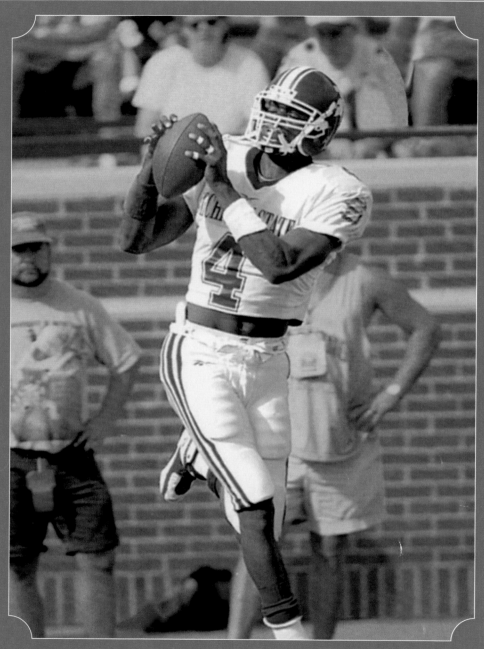

Plaxico Burress grabs a catch during his college career at Michigan State University. In 1999 Plaxico set a Spartans single-season record for touchdown receptions, with 12. He decided to turn pro before his senior year.

Union Military Academy, a prep school in Chesapeake, Virginia, in 1996. Plaxico played football at Fork Union. As a wide receiver, he caught 33 passes for 807 yards and scored 12 touchdowns.

A College Record-Setter

The next year, Plaxico went to Michigan State University. He did not play football at Michigan State during the 1997 season because he still needed to work on his grades. By 1998, however, Plaxico was on Michigan State's football squad. This Big Ten Conference team had a proud football heritage. Playing for the Spartans, he became one of college football's biggest stars.

During the 1998 season, Plaxico started all 12 games. In four of those games he **eclipsed** the 100-yard receiving mark. In one game against Purdue, he had 10 catches for 150 yards. In a game against Notre Dame, he caught an 86-yard pass for a touchdown. In total, he gained 1,013 yards. Plaxico set a Spartans record by catching 65 passes. He also tied a school record by scoring eight touchdowns. The Sports Network selected him for the All–Big Ten Conference first team, and *The Sporting News* ranked him as the fourth best receiver in the country.

The next season, Plaxico beat his own record by catching 66 passes to gain 1,142 yards. He scored 12 touchdowns to set a new Spartans record. Plaxico made the All–Big Ten first team again.

Plaxico's biggest game of his junior year was probably the Citrus Bowl. Playing against the University of Florida on New Year's Day 2000, the Spartans won, 37–34. Plaxico caught 13 passes for 185 yards, scored three touchdowns, and was named the game's Most Valuable Player (MVP).

Following his junior year in college, Plaxico was faced with a decision. Should he play another year with Michigan State or tackle professional football by entering the NFL draft?

CROSS-CURRENTS

To learn more about one of college football's major conferences, check out "The Big Ten." Go to page 48. ▶▶

CROSS-CURRENTS

Read "The NFL Draft" to learn more about how the top college players are chosen by NFL teams each year. Go to page 48. ▶▶

MAKING
THE PROS

In college, Plaxico Burress made his mark with a graceful running style. He proved that he could get downfield quickly, easily leap above defenders, and use his size to his advantage. He was the first player in Spartans history to put together back-to-back 1,000-yard receiving seasons (1998 and 1999). Nobody could deny that he was NFL material.

Plaxico decided to **forgo** his last season of eligibility at Michigan State and enter the 2000 NFL draft. Many teams took an interest in him. There was one problem, however. While in college Plaxico had become known as a player who hated to practice. Most teams thought of that as a lack of maturity. They expected that the prized receiver would grow out of the problem.

Heinz Field Stadium, in Pittsburgh, Pennsylvania, is home to the Steelers, one of football's most successful franchises. As the 2000 NFL draft approached, Steelers head coach Bill Cowher had his eye on Plaxico Burress.

On to the NFL

The Pittsburgh Steelers showed the most interest in Plaxico. The Steel City team had a proud history that included legendary players, such as Pro Football Hall of Fame receivers Lynn Swann and John Stallworth. Although the Steelers had not won a Super Bowl since 1980, they had reached the playoffs many times. The Steelers thought drafting Plaxico could have an immediate positive impact on the team.

Plaxico got off to a rough start with the Steelers, however. He missed a predraft meeting with Steelers head coach Bill Cowher, who had traveled to Michigan State to meet him. Plaxico said he

CROSS-CURRENTS

Read "Men of Steel" to learn about the history of the Pittsburgh Steelers, one of the NFL's most successful teams. Go to page 50. ▶▶

Fleer's rookie card for Plaxico Burress. The Pittsburgh Steelers selected Plaxico in the first round of the 2000 NFL draft and gave him a $5 million signing bonus.

got home late the night before from an out-of-state trip and over-slept, missing the meeting. Cowher said that Plaxico had called, explained what happened, and apologized. The missed meeting did not harm the Steelers' interest in drafting Plaxico. Coach Cowher and Plaxico eventually met and developed a great relationship.

Pittsburgh's Pick

In the 2000 NFL draft, the Steelers had the eighth selection in the first round. Knowing that the Steelers were in prime position to draft a top college player, many other teams tried to persuade the Steelers' management to trade their first-round pick for an established player and let another team take advantage of the draft. The Steelers resisted all these offers and kept their draft pick.

The 2000 draft decision was not easy for the Steelers or their fans. One reason for this was that Plaxico was not the only great player available. Drafting Plaxico would mean not drafting Marshall University's star quarterback Chad Pennington, considered the best quarterback in the draft. It was a tough decision for the Steelers, who felt Pennington could be an NFL quarterback for many years to come. In the end, the Steelers drafted Plaxico on April 15, 2000. Their decision would give their quarterback, Kordell Stewart, a big playmaker to whom to throw. In a *Sports Illustrated* interview, Coach Cowher gave some insight into the team's decision:

> **"We looked at other guys, but he [Burress] was the one guy we felt worthy of that pick. We needed a playmaker, and he was the best playmaker on the board. We looked at what was best for our team, and we felt like Plaxico Burress was a guy we couldn't afford to pass up."**

The Steelers gave Plaxico a $5 million signing bonus. They also gave him something he wanted very dearly—a chance to win the Super Bowl. The Pittsburgh Steelers had a solid reputation for winning. With Plaxico joining the team, the Steelers seemed poised to improve the passing game of their offense. At the time, the Steelers' offense relied heavily on handing the ball to star running back Jerome "The Bus" Bettis and letting him plow his way through defenders on the ground.

Plaxico seemed sold on the Steelers even before they announced his name as their selection. Plaxico described Coach Cowher as an intense man and said he loved that intensity. In addition, he felt the coach could instruct a player on how to be successful. The promising young wide receiver headed to the Steel City to make his NFL dreams come true.

Making the Transition

It is always hard for a player to make the transition from college football to the NFL. The players in the NFL are bigger and more experienced than those on college teams. Rookies have to learn the strengths and weaknesses of the players in the NFL. In Plaxico's case, he had to learn the ways opposing defenders handled themselves. Plaxico also had to understand the Steelers' offense and get used to working with the team's quarterback, Kordell Stewart.

The NFL is a business. The way defenders earn their money and keep their jobs is by stopping players like Plaxico from catching the ball and making big plays. Those defenders take their job very seriously. Many young wide receivers have failed to make it in the NFL.

During a preseason game in 2000 against Dallas, Plaxico made a great diving catch. Seeing what he could do, the Steelers began to get excited about their new receiver.

A Disappointing Rookie Season

Plaxico played well in the first game of the Steelers' 2000 regular season. Playing against the Baltimore Ravens on September 3, he made four catches for 77 yards, including one for 39 yards. That first game, however, was Plaxico's best performance of the season. As the season progressed, he started to drop key passes. In addition, he made a huge mistake during a game against the Jacksonville Jaguars. After hitting the ground as he made a catch, Plaxico got up and spiked the ball on the ground, thinking he had scored a touchdown. He had not, however, scored a touchdown, and the Jaguars knew it. After Plaxico spiked the ball, a Jacksonville player grabbed it. This meant that the Steelers lost the ball. Plaxico's embarrassing turnover was replayed on the Internet and TV sports shows and became the object of jokes on late-night talk shows.

After a short reception, Plaxico Burress is wrapped up by Baltimore Ravens cornerback Chris McAlister in a game in Baltimore, October 29, 2000. Plaxico had a disappointing rookie season, catching just 22 balls and failing to score a single touchdown.

Cleveland Browns defensive back Anthony Henry has Plaxico Burress tightly covered during a game on November 11, 2001. Plaxico had four receptions for 44 yards in the game, which Pittsburgh won in overtime, 15–12.

Soon after, the Steelers' management announced that Plaxico had a serious injury to his right wrist. The injury cut his season short, forcing Plaxico to miss the last four games of the Steelers' 16-game season. Plaxico had to have delicate surgery on his wrist before the end of the season. The team would not know if he had made a full recovery until training camp started in the summer of 2001.

As a result of his right-wrist injury, Plaxico's high hopes for his rookie season were **dashed**. He had only caught 22 passes for 273 yards—way below what the scouts and the Steelers' coaching staff expected. The Steelers, however, still believed Plaxico could be a top player. They were willing to wait and see how he played after recovering from his wrist injury.

Hitting His Stride

By the beginning of the 2001 season, Plaxico was ready to play again. In the Steelers' first game of the season, on September 9, he caught two passes for 24 yards against Jacksonville. It was hardly an offensive explosion, but Plaxico had something to build on.

On October 29, Plaxico had the first 100-yard-receiving game of his NFL career. Playing against the Tennessee Titans, he caught six passes for 151 yards. It was the biggest game of his budding career. A week later, in a game against the Baltimore Ravens, Plaxico scored his first NFL touchdown on a 21-yard pass from quarterback Kordell Stewart. He had another big game against the Ravens later that season on December 16, during which he caught eight passes for 164 yards. Playing against the Cincinnati Bengals on December 30, Plaxico reached another milestone: his first two-touchdown game in the NFL.

Plaxico started all 16 games of the regular season. During the 2001 season, he caught 66 passes for 1,008 yards, his first 1,000-yard-receiving season in the NFL. In four games, he had 100 or more yards receiving. He scored six touchdowns during the regular season. Plaxico also dropped fewer passes. Plaxico's excellent season helped lead the Steelers to a 13–3 season record and first place in the AFC Central Division.

Plaxico looked forward to playing in his first NFL postseason. In the AFC divisional playoff game against the Baltimore Ravens, Plaxico led the Steelers with five receptions for 84 yards and a touchdown. This helped Pittsburgh defeat the Ravens, 27–10. The next week Plaxico caught another five passes, good for 67 yards, in the AFC Championship game against the New England Patriots. But the Steelers lost the game, 24–17.

Although he was disappointed that the Steelers did not make it to the Super Bowl, Plaxico had made it to the NFL playoffs and was sure he would be back.

A jubilant Hines Ward leaps on his teammate Plaxico Burress after Plaxico's 25-yard touchdown catch against the Baltimore Ravens, December 16, 2001. The Steelers won the game, 26–21, and finished the season atop the AFC Central Division with a 13–3 record.

Tragedy Strikes

The off-season turned out to be unexpectedly hard for Plaxico Burress. In March 2002, Plaxico's mother, who was only 49 years old, suddenly became ill with complications from diabetes. As a result of her illness, the lower part of one of her legs had to be amputated. She developed an infection following the amputation and died a few days after the surgery. Plaxico was devastated.

At his mother's funeral Plaxico was asked to deliver the eulogy. He said,

> **"There are three things my mother taught me: Never take anything for granted, always treat others the way you want to be treated, and God won't put anything in front of you that you can't handle."**

Although Plaxico thought he could cope with his mother's death, he had a very hard time dealing with it. He had lost the person who meant the most to him—the one person who always believed in him, the person with whom he hoped to celebrate a Super Bowl championship, and his biggest fan. On top of the loss, his mother's passing gave Plaxico the responsibility of taking care of his younger brothers, Rick and Carlos.

At around the same time, he began living with a group of his childhood friends, some of whom were criminals. After being arrested for public drunkenness, Plaxico knew he had to make big changes in his life. As the start of the 2002 season neared, however, Plaxico was still trying to adjust to life without his mother. His teammates wondered how her death would affect him on the football field.

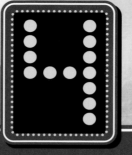

A GIANT STEP

When the Steelers' training camp got under way in late July 2002, Plaxico was still trying to cope with his mother's death. He missed her every day. His mother's passing made him so aware of life's uncertainties that he rededicated himself to the game of football to make the most of the opportunity he had in the NFL.

Plaxico put together a dazzling season in 2002. He started all 16 of the Steelers' games. Over the whole season, Plaxico caught 78 passes to gain 1,325 yards and scored seven touchdowns. With a record of 10 wins, five losses, and a tie in the 2002 regular season, the Steelers won the AFC North Division championship. (Before the season, the American Football Conference had been reorganized. The AFC North had replaced the Central Division.)

Several games stood out for Plaxico. On October 13, he caught eight passes to gain 149 yards, helping Pittsburgh trounce the Cincinnati Bengals, 34–7. On November 10, Plaxico had his best NFL game up to that point. Playing against Atlanta, Plaxico caught nine passes to gain 253 yards—a team record. Plaxico also scored two touchdowns in that game, a 34–34 tie with the Atlanta Falcons.

A Dynamic Duo

When the playoffs began in January 2003, Plaxico and the Steelers were looking forward to continuing their success. In the first round of the playoffs, they beat the Cleveland Browns, 36–33. Plaxico made six catches to gain 100 yards and scored a touchdown. In the same game, another Steelers receiver, Hines Ward, had 104 yards receiving.

With Tampa Bay Buccaneers Dexter Jackson (left) and Dwight Smith in hot pursuit, Plaxico Burress lunges forward for some yards, December 23, 2002. Plaxico grabbed five receptions for 127 yards in the game, a 17–7 Pittsburgh victory.

One-Man Showtime: How's Kobe's Team Doing?

Sports Illustrated

NFL MIDSEASON REPORT

STEELERS
BACK ON TOP
BY PETER KING

THE ROAD TO SUPER BOWL
XXXIX
DR. Z's PICKS

Pittsburgh receivers
Hines Ward and
Plaxico Burress

SPECIAL REPORT
GET OUT AND PLAY
How to get our kids back in shape
BY TIM LAYDEN

www.si.com | AOL Keyword: Sports Illustrated

For several seasons, Pittsburgh's wide receiver tandem of Plaxico Burress and Hines Ward was among the most dangerous in the NFL. This *Sports Illustrated* cover is from 2004.

It was the first time the powerful Steelers had two receivers reach the 100-yard mark in a postseason game since Hall of Famers John Stallworth and Lynn Swann accomplished this feat in Super Bowl XIII in January 1979. To people who had been watching the Steelers all season, the success of both Plaxico and Ward in the playoffs came as no surprise. The two of them made up the best pair of receivers on one team in the NFL in 2002.

In the second round of the playoffs, the Steelers' Super Bowl hopes were dashed when the Tennessee Titans beat them in overtime, 34–31. Plaxico only caught two passes for 62 yards in the losing effort. He was not happy with his team's playoff loss, but he felt that his mother would have been proud of his season.

Plaxico's teammates certainly thought highly of him. Charlie Batch, a backup quarterback for the 2002 Steelers, compared Plaxico to Herman Moore, a receiver he used to play with on the Detroit Lions. Plaxico was often compared to Moore, because both are thin, tall, strong receivers. In a *Football Digest* article, Batch pointed out,

> **"You look at Plaxico and Herman and they're similar in stature, but Plaxico's speed is so much better. He doesn't look like a burner, but he actually is. If you put the ball around him, he'll catch it."**

In the same article, Plaxico's teammate Hines Ward said,

> **"He's a rare receiver, to be that tall and have that power and strength."**

A Tough 2003

Determined to improve his game, Plaxico joined a group of 20 other NFL stars in the summer of 2003 for a special training camp. The training helped Plaxico improve the way he used his speed. It also helped him improve his body control and balance. The camp made Plaxico realize that the greater his success, the more the other teams would come after him.

CROSS-CURRENTS

If you would like to learn more about how teams get into the NFL playoffs, read "Wild Card Teams." Go to page 51. ▶▶

The Steelers hoped to make the playoffs again in 2003, but the team struggled during the regular season. The previous year, the Steelers had replaced quarterback Kordell Stewart with Tommy Maddox. In 2003, with Maddox as the starting quarterback, the Steelers played more of a running game than a passing game. With the team relying on the run, Plaxico had fewer opportunities to make big plays.

It was a disappointing season for both Plaxico and his team. The Steelers won just six games in 2003. With Plaxico coming off back-to-back 1,000-yard-receiving seasons, his 60 catches, 860 yards, and four touchdowns were also a letdown. Needless to say, Steelers fans were not happy with how the team played in 2003.

After the 2003 season, the Steelers drafted quarterback Ben Roethlisberger. The young quarterback had been a star at Miami University of Ohio. Roethlisberger was excited about throwing passes to Plaxico. The Steelers decided to hold a **minicamp** in May 2004. At the minicamp, players could get some practice time in before training camp started in late July, and they could meet their new quarterback.

Plaxico, however, did not show up to the minicamp. He had not told the Steelers that he would not be there. Coach Bill Cowher was furious. Some people thought Plaxico's absence had to do with his contract. Plaxico said that he was unhappy the Steelers had held the camp over Mother's Day weekend. That weekend, Plaxico had gone to spend time with his brothers and pay respects to his late mother.

Steel City Blues

Plaxico explained his actions to Steelers coach Bill Cowher and made up with the Steelers' management before training camp opened in late July. Some people, however, still believed that skipping the mini-camp strained the relationship between the Steelers and Plaxico.

With Ben Roethlisberger as their quarterback, the Pittsburgh Steelers were able to turn things around in 2004. They finished first in the AFC North with a 15–1 record. Plaxico had an up-and-down season in 2004, however. He finished the season as the Steelers' third-best receiver, with 35 catches, 698 yards gained, and a yards-per-reception average of 19.9 yards. He also scored five touchdowns.

Pittsburgh quarterback Tommy Maddox prepares to throw during a game against San Francisco on November 17, 2003. Maddox was less than stellar during the 2003 season, and the Steelers stumbled to a 6–10 record.

New England cornerback Asante Samuel breaks up a potential touchdown pass to Plaxico Burress in the fourth quarter of the AFC Championship game, January 23, 2005. The Patriots ended Pittsburgh's Super Bowl dreams by handing the Steelers a 41–27 loss.

One problem for Plaxico in 2004 was that a hamstring injury forced him to miss five of the team's last six games. Another problem was that the team's strategy had changed. The new quarterback preferred to throw to Plaxico's fellow receiver, Hines Ward. Plaxico also felt that the Steelers relied more on the running game than the passing game.

In the 2004 playoffs, Plaxico contributed to the Steelers' 20–17 win over the New York Jets by catching two passes for 28 yards. He also caught three passes for 37 yards against the New England Patriots in the AFC Championship game. The Steelers, however, lost that game, 41–27.

A Free Agent

During the 2004 season, Pittsburgh Steelers fans wondered whether the Steelers would sign Plaxico to a new contract. Plaxico's contract with the Steelers ended after the season, making him an unrestricted free agent. As an unrestricted free agent, Plaxico could sign a new contract with any NFL team that wanted him.

Shortly after the playoffs, Plaxico announced that he would become a free agent when his contract ended on March 1, 2005. He said that he probably would not return to the Steelers. In spite of his success with the team, Plaxico had some doubts about his future in Pittsburgh. Getting only three or four passes a game was not enough for Plaxico. He felt the Steelers were not giving him much of an opportunity to showcase his talents as a big playmaker. While he said that he didn't have to be the focus of the team's offense, Plaxico felt that he brought talents to the team that the Steelers were overlooking. Steelers quarterback Ben Roethlisberger **lobbied** hard for the team to keep Plaxico, but the quarterback's efforts went nowhere. The Steelers decided not to make Plaxico an offer. They allowed him to leave the team as a free agent.

With his agility and his explosive speed on the field, Plaxico had the potential to become a highly paid NFL player. Several teams showed an interest in Plaxico, including the New York Giants and the Minnesota Vikings. The Giants felt Plaxico would be the perfect target for Eli Manning, the new quarterback they had added in 2004. The Giants were building a reputation for signing talented veteran players who were reaching the peaks of their careers. Plaxico fit right into that category, and the Giants pursued him. As the NFL's unrestricted free agent signing period started on March 2, 2005, the New York news media reported that the Giants were likely to sign Plaxico. The team had made an offer to him.

On March 10, 2005, however, Giants general manager Ernie Accorsi took away the offer for Plaxico. According to Accorsi, the Giants were having too many problems dealing with Plaxico's **agent**. It looked as if Plaxico would not be playing for Big Blue—as the New York Giants were nicknamed—after all. Shortly after the Giants took away the offer, however, Plaxico fired his agent and replaced him with Drew Rosenhaus. Rosenhaus quickly contacted the Giants. One week after claiming they were no longer interested in having Plaxico on their team, the Giants offered him a six-year, $25 million contract. Plaxico signed the contract on March 17, 2005.

A packed house at Giants Stadium in East Rutherford, New Jersey. In March 2005, Plaxico signed with the Giants—and moved into the glare of the New York media spotlight.

A Big Apple Welcome

The Giants were thrilled with their new receiver. A day after Plaxico signed his contract, Giants head coach Tom Coughlin said, on *Giants.com*,

> **"He [Plaxico] makes us a better football team, there's no doubt about that. He is a guy who has an imposing physical presence. And because he does have the ability to be a long ball threat, he is a guy that will force defenses to pay particular attention to where he is."**

Plaxico was excited about joining the Giants. He knew the team wanted to improve its offense by giving Eli Manning better receivers. In a story on *Giants.com*, Plaxico said,

CROSS-CURRENTS

Read "Pro Football in New York City" to learn some history about the Big Apple's NFL teams. Go to page 52. ▶▶

> **"I get an opportunity to go out and play with a great offense. . . . Hopefully, we'll get on the same page and Manning-to-Burress will become a big thing around here. It's going to be fun."**

Before Plaxico went to the Giants' training camp in the summer of 2005, he had one more deal to seal. On June 12, he married his girlfriend of several years, Tiffany Glenn. The couple purchased a home in New Jersey. Everything was in place for Plaxico's **debut** with the New York Giants.

BECOMING AN NFL CHAMP

The New York Giants entered the 2005 season with new energy. Although they had won only six games in 2004, the team seemed ready to improve its game. The Giants lineup included veterans Tiki Barber, Jeremy Shockey, Amani Toomer, Michael Strahan, and Osi Umenyiora; the improving young quarterback, Eli Manning; and an exciting new wide receiver, Plaxico Burress.

A Great Start

Plaxico viewed playing with the Giants as a new beginning for him. He chose to wear the number 17 on his jersey to mark the day he signed with the Giants—March 17, 2005. In his first regular-season

Plaxico Burress, now wearing the uniform of the New York Giants, does a bit of showboating after a reception. Plaxico quickly became a favorite of Giants fans, and he turned in a huge season in 2005.

game with the Giants, Plaxico caught five passes for 76 yards and scored a touchdown against the Arizona Cardinals. The Giants won, 42–19. A few weeks later, he amazed Giants fans by catching 10 passes for 204 yards and scoring two touchdowns, as the Giants beat the St. Louis Rams, 44–24.

Plaxico was becoming Eli Manning's favorite target. The game against the Rams showed how well Plaxico was working with the quarterback. Manning threw a pass up the middle, and it looked as though the ball was going to be intercepted. Plaxico, however, saw where the ball was going, ran in front of the Rams defender to make the catch, and raced into the end zone for a touchdown. In a *Sports Illustrated* article, the team's general manager, Ernie Accorsi, said of the play,

Giants quarterback Eli Manning had struggled in 2004, his rookie season. But the addition of Plaxico Burress to New York's receiver corps gave him a big new weapon for the passing game.

"You need a lot of anticipation to make that throw. Most young quarterbacks won't throw the ball unless they know a guy is open. But Eli has a great feel for Plaxico. He's smart enough to know this guy will help him play better.**"**

In *Sports Illustrated*, Eli Manning added,

"I can just look at Plaxico's body movement and know when he's going to make a cut.**"**

Plaxico liked the way the Giants were using him. He also liked that his teammates were beginning to rely on him to make big plays. Plaxico's teammates were surprised to find that he was soft-spoken in the locker room. In a *New York Times* interview, Plaxico said,

"I've never really been a vocal guy.**"**

Getting Comfortable in New York

With his success in New York, Plaxico opened up a bit more about the difficulty he had dealing with his mother's death while he was with the Steelers and the peace he eventually found. He feels that his mother still pushes him to do his best. In the *New York Times* interview, he said,

"Some days I wish I could hug her and kiss her. . . . That's unfortunate that I can't, but I still talk to her all the time, and she talks to me. It's one of those things that really made me believe in spiritual contact.**"**

During the 2005 season, Plaxico made dramatic catches as well as several blocks to help running back Tiki Barber score key touchdowns. He also contributed to the Giants' 27–17 win over their rivals, the Philadelphia Eagles, by catching six passes for 113 yards and scoring a touchdown.

The Giants' 2005 record was 11–5, placing the team first in the NFC East. Plaxico had a great season, with 76 receptions for 1,214 yards and seven touchdowns. The Giants, however, lost in the first round of

CROSS-CURRENTS

Read "Good Wishes in Super Times" to learn how Plaxico's Steelers team-mates supported his Super Bowl dreams. Go to page 53. ▶▶

the playoffs to the Carolina Panthers. In spite of the loss, Plaxico was not discouraged. He felt that one day he would get his chance to play in the Super Bowl.

Only Breaking Even

With only an 8–8 record, the Giants had a disappointing season. Although Plaxico played with a painful groin injury most of the season, he again had a strong season. He caught 63 passes for 988 yards and scored 10 touchdowns.

There was one play, however, that bothered Plaxico more than any other in 2006. In a game against Tennessee, with Plaxico still hampered by his injury, Titans cornerback Adam "Pacman" Jones rushed in front of him and intercepted a pass from Eli Manning. The Giants lost that game, 24–21. In spite all the big plays Plaxico made in 2006, that interception stood out in his mind.

In the 2006 playoffs, the Giants played Philadelphia in the NFC wild card game. Plaxico made five catches for 89 yards and scored two touchdowns. However, the Giants lost the close game to the Eagles, 23–20.

Although the 2006 season ended too soon for him, Plaxico and his wife, Tiffany, rejoiced just a few days later on January 13, 2007, when their son Elijah was born. Following Elijah's birth, Plaxico showed a new happiness both on the field and off.

CROSS-CURRENTS

Read "A Proud and Grateful Hometown" to find out about some of the good things Plaxico has done in Virginia Beach. Go to page 53. ▶▶

High Hopes

During the off-season, Plaxico stayed in touch with Eli Manning. The two talked on the phone two or three times a week. Plaxico and Manning got together often, without the pressure of team meetings, practices, and reporters swarming around them. They wanted to develop a **rapport** off the field that would make them more in tune with each other on the field during games.

Plaxico was ready to have a great season when the Giants' 2007 training camp opened at the end of July. During a preseason game,

Plaxico Burress makes a leaping touchdown catch in front of Dallas Cowboys safety Patrick Watkins in a game at Texas Stadium in Irving, Texas, on October 23, 2006. The Giants came out on top, 36–22, but managed to win only seven other games during the season.

however, he appeared to have sprained his right ankle. He continued to play, and the Giants were not concerned about the injury, which they felt was relatively minor.

When the regular season started, Plaxico had a solid first two games, scoring three touchdowns in the first game against the Dallas Cowboys and one touchdown in the second game against the Green Bay Packers. The Giants, however, lost both those games.

Playing Through the Pain

In the second game of the season, Plaxico seemed to have sprained his ankle again. After losing the first two games of the 2007 season, the Giants knew they could not afford to lose Plaxico to injury. His ankle, however, was more seriously hurt than the Giants had first

Plaxico Burress straight-arms Andre Dyson of the New York Jets en route to a touchdown, October 7, 2007. Behind Plaxico's 124 receiving yards, the Giants won the battle of Big Apple teams, 35–24.

thought. It turned out that Plaxico had torn a **ligament** in his right ankle. Plaxico considered having surgery to fix the ligament, but the recovery time would probably have sidelined him for the rest of the season. He decided to keep playing.

Doctors recommended rest and advised against strenuous practice. During the week, Plaxico did light jogging to help build up his ankle and spent hours catching passes thrown by a machine. When he played, Plaxico started each game slowly, not knowing what to expect from his right ankle. As the game progressed, he felt stronger and was able to contribute more. He helped the Giants make several big comebacks in games against the New York Jets and the Washington Redskins. Once he was able to make the adjustments he needed to play on his sore ankle, Plaxico put together big second halves to help his team win the games. In an article in the *Virginian-Pilot*, Plaxico is quoted as saying,

"I got frustrated at times, but I stayed faithful within myself and went out and competed the best I could. It wasn't always what I wanted it to be, but I didn't make excuses, didn't complain. I just went out and played the hand I was dealt."

Plaxico was an inspiration to his teammates, who battled alongside him all season to reach the playoffs. His injury actually had an unexpected benefit that made him a better player. Unable to practice, Plaxico spent hours watching game films and studying the Giants' playbook. Studying football in that way opened his eyes to things he never had time to analyze before. Coach Tom Coughlin said of his play in 2007,

"The amazing thing is his number of mental errors has been at an absolute minimum."

Even with his painful ankle injury, Plaxico still had a great season, starting all 16 games, making 70 catches for 1,025 yards, and scoring 12 touchdowns. The Giants won 10 games. This was good enough to finish in second place in the NFC East and make it to the playoffs as a wild-card team.

Plaxico Burress celebrates his go-ahead touchdown reception late in the fourth quarter of Super Bowl XLII, February 3, 2008. The Giants hung on to win the game, 17–14.

A Perfect Playoff Record

In the first round of the playoffs, the Giants beat the Tampa Bay Buccaneers, 24–14. In the divisional playoffs, the Giants faced the Dallas Cowboys. The Giants had already lost to Dallas twice during the 2007 season. Many people did not think they had much of a chance of beating the Cowboys in the playoffs. The Giants, however, outplayed the Cowboys and won, 21–17.

Plaxico's injury limited his contributions in the first two playoff games. However, his presence on the field distracted the Giants' opponents, forcing them to pay attention to him and not guard other Giants receivers as heavily.

The Giants faced the tough Green Bay Packers in the NFC Championship game on January 20, 2008. In spite of the ankle injury—which did not allow him to practice the week before the game—and subzero temperatures in Green Bay, Wisconsin, Plaxico played one of his best games ever in the championship contest. By catching a team-record 11 passes to gain 151 yards, Plaxico helped the Giants beat the Packers, 23–20, in overtime. The victory sent the Giants to the Super Bowl.

On February 3, 2008, the Giants played Super Bowl XLII against the undefeated and heavily favored New England Patriots. With just 35 seconds left in the game, Plaxico caught a pass for the winning touchdown. The Giants won the Super Bowl, 17–14. Plaxico and his teammates had earned their championship rings.

CROSS-CURRENTS

Read "A Giant Celebration" to learn about the ticker-tape parade that New York City held for its Super Bowl champs. Go to page 54. ▶▶

The Giants' victory made an impact throughout the country. It was seen as a triumph for underdogs everywhere, for everyone who refused to give up in the face of nearly impossible odds. There were many parades and celebrations to mark the victory. The one that meant the most to Plaxico was the one held in his hometown of Virginia Beach. There, Green Run High School officially retired Plaxico's number 5 football jersey and declared Plaxico Burress Day.

One of the people at the celebration was Plaxico's former high school football coach, Cadillac Harris, who said proudly,

❝He's really connected all the dots. He never lost who he is.❞

A Brief History of the Super Bowl

The Super Bowl is the championship game of the National Football League (NFL). It is one of the biggest sporting events in the United States. Played once a year, the game always takes place on a Sunday in January or February—Super Bowl Sunday—and many fans hold parties to celebrate pro football's main event. The game is usually the most watched television broadcast of the year. As the final game of the NFL playoffs, the Super Bowl determines which team is the league's champion for that year. The teams that play in the Super Bowl are the champions of the NFL's two conferences—the National Football Conference (NFC) and the American Football Conference (AFC).

The Super Bowl was born when two football leagues in the United States merged. The National Football League was founded in 1920. Over the years, several rival leagues had come and gone, but none threatened the NFL until the American Football League (AFL) started in 1960. Unlike other rival leagues, the AFL had enough money to compete for players—and fans. Several major college football stars decided to play in the AFL rather than in the NFL.

New England Patriots quarterback Tom Brady holds up the Vince Lombardi Trophy following the Patriots' 32–29 victory over the Carolina Panthers in Super Bowl XXXVIII, February 1, 2004. The Super Bowl has been played each year since 1967.

Each time a big-name college player signed with an AFL team, the upstart league attracted more and more fans. Faced with a fierce and well-funded rival, the NFL started merger talks with the AFL in early 1966, in an attempt to bring the AFL teams into the NFL. A merger agreement was announced in June 1966, but the deal was not completed until 1970.

On January 15, 1967, the top teams from the two leagues met in a championship game for the first time. The game was called the AFL-NFL World Championship Game. In the first championship game between the NFL and the AFL, the NFL's powerful Green Bay Packers easily defeated the AFL's Kansas City Chiefs. The next year, the Packers beat the AFL's Oakland Raiders. After the Packers' back-to-back wins, some people worried that the AFL teams might never be as good as the NFL teams. In the third championship game, however, the AFL's New York Jets upset the heavily favored NFL's Baltimore Colts, 16–7, and the competitiveness of the AFL was never questioned again. Pro football's championship game has been officially called the Super Bowl ever since this game. The Super Bowl championship trophy is now called the Vince Lombardi Trophy, named after the Packers' legendary coach who won the first two championship games.

(Go back to page 5.)

What Is a Wide Receiver?

A wide receiver—also called a wideout—is a key member of a football team's offensive squad. When the offensive team lines up for a play, the wide receivers are the offensive players standing closest to the sidelines. The main job of the wide receiver is to catch passes thrown by the quarterback and score touchdowns. Coaches develop plays for the wide receivers to run to get past the opponent's defenders and catch the ball. Wide receivers are among the fastest and most agile players on a team. A wide receiver must be able to hold onto the ball when it is thrown to him to complete the play and gain yards. Once a wide receiver catches the ball, he runs downfield to gain as many yards as possible. If he can make it into the end zone, he scores a touchdown. Along the way, the other team tries to tackle the wide receiver before he gains too many yards for his team.

Some wide receivers are so fast that they outrun the other team's defenders and stay in the open to catch the ball. It is important for a quarterback to have a clear view when throwing to a wide receiver, so it helps if a wide receiver is tall.

(Go back to page 9.)

The Big Ten

Toward the end of the 1800s, one of the problems in college sports was that some college teams used professional athletes and nonstudents to give them an edge. In 1896, the Western Conference was founded to make rules for college sports. One of its first rules was that only full-time students with passing grades could participate in intercollegiate sports at its schools.

By 1917, ten colleges had joined the conference, and people were calling it the "Big Ten." Through the years, several colleges joined and left the conference. At one point, when the conference consisted of only nine schools, it was known as the Big Nine. From 1950 until 1990, it consisted of ten schools, and it has been known as the Big Ten ever since. The conference membership remained the same for 40 years, until 1990, when its members voted to add an eleventh school. In spite of the new addition, the conference is still called the Big Ten.

Today, Big Ten schools compete in a variety of men's and women's sports, including football, basketball, and baseball. The conference's members are the University of Illinois, Indiana University, the University of Iowa, the University of Michigan, Michigan State University, the University of Minnesota, Northwestern University, Ohio State University, Purdue University, the University of Wisconsin, and Pennsylvania State University. Penn State is the newest member.

(Go back to page 15.) ◀◀

The NFL Draft

Each year, the National Football League (NFL) holds a draft in which its teams choose new young players. Most of the players who take part in the draft are top college football players who have played the maximum number of years of college football that they are allowed. Some top college football players choose to enter the NFL draft before they have run out of college-level playing time. Players have many reasons for entering the NFL draft before finishing college. One big reason is that pro teams are often willing to pay huge amounts of money to the top young football players. Another reason is the danger involved in playing football. If a college football player wants to turn pro—and thinks he is good enough to play in the NFL—he may want to go for it as soon as possible. If he is injured in his last season of college football, his NFL dreams may be shattered forever.

The NFL draft, which began in 1936, was the idea of Bert Bell. Bell was an owner of an NFL team, and he was also a former league commissioner. In the NFL draft, the teams with the worst records in the league get the first picks of the young players, and the teams with better records get later picks. This system allows the weaker teams to get the better players and make their lineups stronger. According to the rules of the draft, however, a team with a better record can get an earlier draft pick by trading for it. The stronger team can give a player to a weaker team in return for the weaker team's rank in the draft.

One reason that the NFL uses this draft system is to keep the league competitive. Before the draft was started, a player could sign with any team that wanted him. Naturally, all the players wanted to join the best teams, and the best teams took the best players. Under this system, the strong got stronger and the weak got weaker. Fans would lose interest in the weaker teams, because those teams could not get the players they needed to improve. The draft makes it possible for a losing team to become a winner.

Over the years, more than 10,000 players have been selected through the NFL draft. Scouts from NFL teams travel around the country watching college players perform so their teams can decide which players to select in the draft.

Linebacker Jordon Dizon of the University of Colorado demonstrates his leaping ability at the NFL scouting combine, February 25, 2008. Each year, the NFL invites top college prospects to the combine before the league's draft.

(Go back to page 15.)

Men of Steel

The Pittsburgh Steelers are one of pro football's most successful teams. The team has won five Super Bowls, six conference championships, and eighteen division championships. Seventeen Steelers are in the Pro Football Hall of Fame, in Canton, Ohio. One of the NFL's oldest franchises, the team entered the league in 1933. At first, the team was called the Pirates. Its name was changed in 1940 to the Steelers, a reference to Pittsburgh's many steel mills. The Rooney family has owned the team since its beginning.

The Steelers tied for first place in 1947 with the Philadelphia Eagles, but they lost 21–0 in a playoff game against the Eagles. That was the last time the Steelers made the playoffs for 25 years. In 1969, the Steelers hired Coach Chuck Noll. Between 1969 and 1974, Noll drafted Charles "Mean Joe" Greene, one of the game's great defensive players; quarterback Terry Bradshaw; running back Franco Harris; and wide receivers Lynn Swann and John Stallworth. These players made up one of pro football's greatest lineups. Between 1974 and 1980, the Pittsburgh Steelers dominated the NFL. The Steelers became the first team to win four Super Bowls.

In the early 1980s, the Steelers' championship players began retiring. In 1992, Noll retired, and Bill Cowher took over for him. Cowher led the Steelers to victory in Super Bowl XL in 2006. (Go back to page 17.) ◄◄

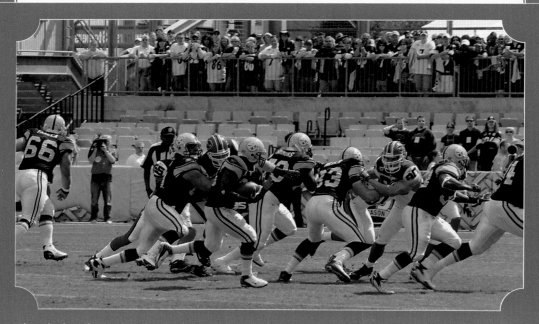

The Pittsburgh Steelers battle the Buffalo Bills at Heinz Field Stadium on September 16, 2007. The Steelers are a storied club. They dominated pro football in the 1970s, winning four Super Bowls in six years.

Wild Card Teams

When the NFL merged with the American Football League (AFL) in 1970, the league divided into two conferences, the American Football Conference (AFC) and the National Football Conference (NFC). Each of the conferences had three divisions, and the team with the best record in each division went to the playoffs. To even out the playoff schedule, a fourth playoff team—called the wild card—had to be added in each conference.

The Original Wild Card Spot

League officials decided that the fourth playoff spot would go to the team with the best record in the conference that did not finish first in its division. In other words, within each conference, the second-place team that compiled the best record earned the wild card spot in the playoffs. In each conference, the wild card team would play its first-round game against the team with the best record, unless that team was from the same division. In that case, the wild card would play the team with the second-best record.

A Second Wild Card Spot

In 1978, the NFL's playoff format changed with the addition of a second wild card spot in each conference. With an additional wild card, the three division-winning teams did not have to play in the first round of the playoffs. The two wild card teams played, and the winner went on to play either the first or second seed (depending on whether they were division rivals) in the next round. In 1981, three seasons after this change, the Oakland Raiders became the first wild card team to win a Super Bowl, defeating the Philadelphia Eagles, 27–10, in Super Bowl XV.

A Third Wild Card Spot

In 1990, the NFL expanded the playoffs again, adding a third wild card spot. Over the next few years, two wild card teams managed to win the Super Bowl: the Denver Broncos (Super Bowl XXXII, in 1998) and the Baltimore Ravens (Super Bowl XXXV, in 2001).

Wild Card Spots Today

The NFL reorganized its two conferences in 2002, expanding both the AFC and NFC to four divisions. Today, the division winners each earn a playoff spot, as do two wild card teams in each conference. Many wild card teams do not do well in the NFL playoffs. One reason for this is that they usually have to play their postseason games on the road. Another reason is that the division winners are usually better teams. Wild cards, however, sometime shock the pro football world. In 2006, the Pittsburgh Steelers became the fourth wild card to win the Super Bowl. The next year, the New York Giants became the fifth wild card Super Bowl winner.

(Go back to page 29.)

Pro Football in New York City

How would Plaxico Burress fit into New York City's media-driven sports scene? Plaxico was a big playmaker. The New York Giants have had many big-name stars over the years, so he had a lot to live up to. Plaxico's **flamboyant** style of play seemed to be just what Giants fans craved.

The New York Football Giants

The New York Football Giants, as they were first known, entered the NFL in 1925. The team was owned by Tim Mara, who paid the $500 needed to get the Giants into the NFL. The Giants wasted no time getting the biggest football star of the time—the legendary Jim Thorpe—to play on their 1925 squad. The Giants won their first championship in 1927. Between 1933 and 1947, the Giants made it to the championship game eight times. They won twice, in 1934 and 1938. One of the team's big stars during that period was Hall of Fame center Mel Hein.

Big-name Players

The Giants' big-name players in the late 1950s and early 1960s included Frank Gifford, Y. A. Tittle, Sam Huff, Del Shofner, and Roosevelt Brown. From 1958 to 1963, the Giants played in five of the six championship games but did not win any of them. The 1958 NFL Championship game, which the Giants lost to the Baltimore Colts in overtime, 23–17, is considered by many the greatest pro football game ever played. This game helped send the popularity of pro football soaring. In later years, stars like Harry Carson, Phil Simms, and Lawrence Taylor all kept the spotlight on the Giants. The team won Super Bowl XXI in 1987 and Super Bowl XXV in 1991 before winning Super Bowl XLII in 2008.

The New York Jets

New York City has another pro football team besides the Giants. New York's other football team started out in the AFL in 1960 as the New York Titans. It changed its name to the Jets in 1963. Like the Giants in Super Bowl XLII , the Jets went into Super Bowl III in 1969 as underdogs. The AFL's New York Jets were playing the NFL's powerful Baltimore Colts. Just as Plaxico predicted that the Giants would beat the undefeated New England Patriots in Super Bowl XLII, Jets quarterback Joe Namath predicted that the Jets would win Super Bowl III. As happened when Plaxico and the Giants beat the Patriots in 2008, the Jets surprised many people when they won the Super Bowl in 1969.

(Go back to page 35.)

Good Wishes in Super Times

In 2005, the year Plaxico Burress left the Pittsburgh Steelers—the only NFL team he had ever been with—the Steelers won Super Bowl XL. The Steelers had come close to reaching the Super Bowl when Plaxico was with them, but they never made it while he was on the team.

Many of his former Steelers' teammates felt bad that Plaxico had missed a chance to go to the Super Bowl during his time in Pittsburgh. When Plaxico's new team, the New York Giants, made it to the Super Bowl a few years later, many of his former teammates were rooting for him to win the big one. Leading the supporters was his former head coach with the Steelers, Bill Cowher. Plaxico said his former coach told him that he deserved to be in the Super Bowl and should enjoy all the fanfare surrounding the game. Plaxico said, "He was just telling me, Hey, man, don't let it get away. Go get that ring." Other former teammates supported him as well, including Hines Ward, Jerome Bettis, Ike Taylor, and Casey Hampton. All of them wanted to see Plaxico win a Super Bowl ring. (Go back to page 40.) ◀◀

A Proud and Grateful Hometown

Long before Plaxico Burress ever played on a winning Super Bowl team, he would return to his hometown to visit family and friends, and to help the community. He made an annual trip to Virginia Beach, Virginia, every Thanksgiving—even though it was in the middle of football season—to give out turkey and ham that he donated to the community's disadvantaged families.

Plaxico also funded scholarships at Green Run High School for students attending his **alma mater**. There was no doubt that when his team got into Super Bowl XLII, many people in Virginia Beach would be watching the game and rooting for their hometown hero.

When the Giants won, the news media focused on New York City and New Jersey, the Giants' home turf. While there was plenty of excitement in those places, Virginia Beach was also bursting with pride and joy. The town could not pass up this opportunity to honor one of its own and scheduled Plaxico Burress Day for April 12, 2008, at the Sandler Center for the Performing Arts. The Green Run High School band played at the ceremony and all the town's dignitaries were on hand to honor Plaxico for his gridiron heroics and his charity work. Plaxico was touched by the outpouring of support and spent hours after the ceremony greeting those who attended and signing autographs. (Go back to page 40.) ◀◀

A Giant Celebration

After the New York Giants' stunning upset of the New England Patriots in Super Bowl XLII, there was only one thing left to do: Hold a ticker-tape parade in New York City.

Ticker-tape Parades

Ticker-tape parades are usually held in large cities, where tall buildings form a "canyon." People pack the streets, hang out building windows, cheer wildly, and throw shredded paper and confetti in what looks like a blizzard. With bands playing, honorees ride on floats and in convertibles with the tops down, waving to the adoring crowds. In New York City, these ticker-tape extravaganzas usually run from lower Broadway through Manhattan's financial district along a route known as the Canyon of Heroes.

Lady Liberty's Arrival

The first ticker-tape parade was held in New York City in 1886. After the dedication of the Statue of Liberty, a spontaneous celebration broke out. Workers at brokerage companies in lower Manhattan started throwing ticker tape out of office windows to celebrate Lady Liberty's arrival as a gift from France. The ticker tape came out of machines the companies used to get updates on the latest stock prices. Today stock-price updates come by computer, so shredded paper is used to shower parade honorees. After the ticker-tape celebration for the Statue of Liberty, New York City officials realized that parades could be staged to honor heads of state as well as those who had made great accomplishments. Through the years, dignitaries from around the nation and the world have been honored with ticker-tape parades. The largest ticker-tape parade ever given in New York is believed to have been for General Douglas MacArthur after his return from the Korean War in 1951.

Honoring Sports Stars

Sports stars, such as Olympian Jesse Owens, golfer Ben Hogan, and tennis great Althea Gibson, have been saluted with parades in New York City. Many New York sports teams have been honored with parades, as well. Ticker-tape parades have been given eight times for baseball's New York Yankees and three times for the New York Mets. Baseball's New York Giants (now based in San Francisco) were honored with a ticker-tape parade in 1954, and hockey's New York Rangers got a parade when they won the Stanley Cup in 1994.

The New York Giants First

Although they had won the Super Bowl in the past, pro football's New York Giants finally got their first ticker-tape parade on February 5, 2008.

(Go back to page 45.)

Throngs of New Yorkers line the Canyon of Heroes on Broadway for a ticker-tape parade honoring the Super Bowl champion New York Giants, February 5, 2008.

1977   Plaxico Burress is born on August 12, in Virginia Beach, Virginia.

1992   Starts his high school sports career.

1998   Plays in his first game for Michigan State on August 29.

2000   Plaxico stars in the Citrus Bowl on January 1.

Plaxico enters the NFL draft, and is selected by the Pittsburgh Steelers in the first round (eighth overall) on April 15.

Plaxico plays in his first NFL game against the Baltimore Ravens on September 3.

2001   Records his first two-touchdown game in the NFL against the Cincinnati Bengals on December 30.

2002   Plaxico's mother, Adelaide Vicki Burress, dies in March.

Plaxico catches 78 passes for 1,325 yards and seven touchdowns, helping the Steelers to reach the AFC Championship game.

2004   Injuries limit Plaxico to 11 games; he catches just 35 passes.

2005   Plaxico's contract with the Steelers expires, and he signs with the New York Giants as a free agent on March 17.

Plaxico marries Tiffany Glenn on June 12.

Plaxico catches 76 passes for 1,214 yards with the Giants.

2006   Scores ten touchdowns in the regular season, and helps the Giants reach the playoffs.

2007   Plaxico and his wife have a baby boy, Elijah, on January 13.

Plaxico catches 12 touchdowns, the most of his career, in helping the Giants earn a wild card playoff spot.

2008   Scores the winning touchdown in Super Bowl XLII, as the New York Giants upset the New England Patriots, 17–14, on February 3.

1995   Rated the best receiver in the country by *Scholastic Sports.*

Named a *Parade* magazine, *Prep Football Report*, and *National Recruiting Advisor* All-American.

Named to the All-State basketball second team.

Wins the state title for the 300 intermediate hurdles as a high school senior.

2000   Named MVP of the Citrus Bowl (Michigan State defeats University of Florida) on January 1.

2001   Has his first 1,000-yard receiving season in the NFL.

2002   Makes nine catches for a Steelers team record 253 yards in a single game on November 10.

Has his second 1,000-yard receiving season in the NFL.

2005   Named NFC Offensive Player of the Week for his play against the St. Louis Rams.

Has his third 1,000-yard receiving season in the NFL.

2007   Has the first three-touchdown game of his career on September 9.

Has the fourth 1,000-yard receiving season of his career.

2008   Scores the winning touchdown against the New England Patriots to help the Giants win Super Bowl XLII.

Green Run High School retires his number 5 football jersey as part of Plaxico Burress Day in Virginia Beach, Virginia, on April 12.

Career Statistics

NFL Regular-Season Career Stats

Season	Team	G	GS	Receiving			
				Rec	Yds	Avg	TD
2007	New York Giants	16	16	70	1,025	14.6	12
2006	New York Giants	15	15	63	988	15.7	10
2005	New York Giants	16	15	76	1,214	16.0	7
2004	Pittsburgh Steelers	11	11	35	698	19.9	5
2003	Pittsburgh Steelers	16	16	60	860	14.3	4
2002	Pittsburgh Steelers	16	15	78	1,325	17.0	7
2001	Pittsburgh Steelers	16	16	66	1,008	15.3	6
2000	Pittsburgh Steelers	12	9	22	273	12.4	0
TOTAL		116	113	470	7,391	15.7	51

NFL Postseason Career Receiving Stats

Season	Team	G	GS	Rec	Yds	Avg	TD
2007	New York Giants	4	4	18	221	12.3	1
2006	New York Giants	1	1	5	89	17.8	2
2005	New York Giants	1	1	0	0	0.0	0
2004	Pittsburgh Steelers	2	2	5	65	13.0	1
2002	Pittsburgh Steelers	2	2	8	162	20.3	1
2001	Pittsburgh Steelers	2	2	10	151	15.1	1
TOTAL		12	12	46	688	14.9	6

Books

Benson, Michael. *The Good, the Bad, and the Ugly New York Giants: Heart-pounding, Jaw-dropping, and Gut-wrenching Moments from New York Giants History*. Chicago: Triumph Books, 2007.

Daily News. *Blue Miracle: New York Giants 2008 Super Bowl Champions*. Champaign, IL: Sports Publishing LLC, 2008.

Director, Roger. *I Dream in Blue: Life, Death, and the New York Giants*, revised ed. New York: Harper Paperback, 2008.

New York Post. *Road Warriors: The New York Giants Incredible 2007 Championship Season*. Chicago: Triumph Books, 2008.

Palmer, Ken. *Game of My Life New York Giants: Memorable Stories of Giants Football*. Champaign, IL: Sports Publishing LLC, 2008.

Schwartz, Paul. *Tales from the New York Giants Sidelines*, updated September 1, 2007, edition. Champaign, IL: Sports Publishing LLC, 2008.

Whittingham, Richard. *What Giants They Were*. Chicago: Triumph Books, 2000.

Web Sites

http://bigten.cstv.com/

This is the official site of the Big Ten Conference. Visitors can find historical information about sporting events at Big Ten schools and biographies of past stars, including their records as college athletes.

http://msuspartans.com

This site contains the latest information about Michigan State University sports, plus historical information about the teams and athletes who have played for the school, including Plaxico Burress.

http://sportsillustrated.cnn.com/football/nfl/

This site combines resources of *Sports Illustrated* and CNN. It contains the latest information about the NFL, plus historical facts about all teams and players in the league.

http://www.giants.com

The official New York Giants Web site is filled with historical and statistical information about the Giants and all their players, team and individual records, and news updates.

http://www.nfl.com

The official site of the National Football League has breaking news about teams in the NFL and information on past games and seasons. It also includes records, highlights, player bios, team histories, Super Bowl history, season wrap-ups, and upcoming schedules.

http://www.steelers.com

The official site of the Pittsburgh Steelers contains historical information about the Steelers and their former and current players with record-setting performances, recaps, and news updates.

The Web sites mentioned in this book were active at the time of publication. The publisher is not responsible for Web sites that have changed their addresses or discontinued operation since the date of publication. The publisher will review and update the Web site addresses each time the book is reprinted.

agent—a person whose job it is to represent someone else, such as a professional athlete, in negotiations.

alma mater—a school from which one has graduated.

dashed—ruined; destroyed.

debut—first appearance.

eclipsed—surpassed, as a record.

flamboyant—flashy in performance or behavior.

forgo—give up; do without.

grueling—exceedingly difficult and demanding.

hampered—got in the way of; held back.

ligament—a tough band of tissue that connects the ends of bones to one another.

lobbied—pressed for; advocated.

minicamp—a special training camp for football players that is usually held in the spring or early summer.

quarterback—the player on a football team who tells the team what play they are running and moves the ball to a running back or receiver after the snap.

rapport—an understanding, a sense of getting along well with someone.

reiterated—repeated, either in spoken or written language.

touchdown—in football, the carrying or catching of the ball beyond the opponent's goal line that is worth six points.

page 6 "He's got such long arms. . . ." Associated Press, "Giants Top Receiver Thinks Teammates Match Up Well with Moss and Company," ESPN.com (January 26, 2008). http://sports.espn.go.com/nfl/news/story?id=3215952.

page 9 "I am going to say it again, . . ." Tom Canavan, "Plaxico Burress Has Come a Long Way," Associated Press (January 30, 2008). http://www.wtopnews.com/?nid=119&sid=1335382.

page 12 "My grandma was sort of a rock, . . ." Tom Canavan, "Plaxico Burress Has Come a Long Way."

page 13 "My grandmother would actually leave . . ." Rich Radford, "Plaxico Burress: Receiver's Name Hasn't Caught On, But His Game Has," *Virginian-Pilot* (September 30, 1994). http://scholar.lib.vt.edu/VA-news/VA-Pilot/issues/1994/vp940930/09300650.htm.

page 19 "We looked at other guys, . . ." "Help for Kordell," CNNSI.com (April 15, 2000). http://sportsillustrated.cnn.com/football/nfl/2000/nfldraft/news/2000/04/15/steelers_burress_ap.

page 25 "There are three things my mother taught me . . ." Mike Garafolo, "Plax's Healing Process," nj.com (January 6, 2008). http://www.nj.com/giants/index.ssf/2008/01/plaxs_healing_process.html.

page 29 "You look at Plaxico and Herman . . ." Ed Bouchette, "The next big thing: Pittsburgh's Plaxico Burress is on the verge of becoming one of the most explosive wideouts in the game," *Football Digest* (November 2003). http://findarticles.com/p/articles/mi_m0FCL/is_3_33/ai_108784456/print.

page 29 "He's a rare receiver. . . ." Bouchette, "The next big thing."

page 35 "He makes us a better football team, . . ." Michael Eisen, "Giants Sign WR Plaxico Burress," Giants.com (March 18, 2005). http://giants.com/news/eisen/story.asp?story_id=6058&print=yes.

page 35 "I get an opportunity . . ." Michael Eisen, "Giants Sign WR Plaxico Burress."

page 39 "You need a lot of anticipation . . ." Jeffri Chadiha, "A Change For The Better," *Sports Illustrated* (October 31, 2005). http://vault.sportsillustrated.cnn.com/vault/article/magazine/MAG1105575/1/index.htm.

page 39 "I can just look at . . ." Chadiha, "A Change For The Better."

page 39 "I've never really . . ." John Branch, "Burress Proving to Be Quite a Catch," *New York Times* (November 13, 2005). http://www.nytimes.com/2005/11/13/sports/football/13giants.html.

page 39 "Some days I wish . . ." Branch, "Burress Proving to Be Quite a Catch."

page 43 "I got frustrated . . ." Tom Robinson, "Good Season Has Erased Bad Attitude for Burress," *Virginian-Pilot* (January 31, 2008). http://hamptonroads.com/2008/01/good-season-has-erased-bad-attitude-burress.

page 43 "The amazing thing is . . ." Robinson, "Good Season Has Erased Bad Attitude for Burress."

page 45 "He's really connected all the dots. . . ." John Streit, "Beach Holds 'Plaxico Burress Day,' Retires NFL Star's Green Run Jersey," *Virginian-Pilot* (April 12, 2008). http://hamptonroads.com/2008/04/beach-holds-plaxico-burress-day-retires-nfl-stars-green-run-jersey.

page 53 "He was just telling me, . . ." Ed Bouchette, "Burress Finally Gets to Reach for the Ring," *Pittsburgh Post-Gazette* (January 30, 2008). http://www.post-gazette.com/pg/08030/853249-66.stm?cmpid=steelers.xml.

Robert Grayson is an award-winning former daily newspaper reporter. He has interviewed and written stories about professional football players for *Pro Football Preview, Sports Collectors Digest,* and *Football Card News,* among others. His sports and lifestyle stories have appeared in numerous magazines, including *NBA Hoop,* the *New York Yankees* magazine, *Family Weekly,* and *Grit.* An avid cat lover, he has written a series of features about cats and dogs in the movies for animal companion magazines and Web sites and wrote an essay for the anthology *Pet Stories across America: Lessons Animals Teach Us.*

PICTURE CREDITS

page

5: Orlando Sentinel/MCT

7: Philadelphia Inquirer/MCT

8: Ben Liebenberg/NFL/Getty Images

11: Chris McGrath/Getty Images

12: T&T/IOA Photos

14: Press Pass/SPCS

17: Tom Murphy VII/T&T/IOA Photos

18: Fleer/NMI

21: George Bridges/KRT

22: Ed Suba Jr./Akron Beacon Journal/KRT

24: George Bridges/KRT

27: John Raoux/Orlando Sentinel/KRT

28: Sports Illustrated/NMI

31: Contra Costa Times/KRT

32: George Bridges/KRT

34: Motorcycle Ride/T&T/IOA Photos

37: Chris McGrath/Getty Images

38: William E. Amatucci/NFL/WireImage

41: Fort Worth Star-Telegram/MCT

42: Thomas A. Ferrara/Newsday/MCT

44: NFL/SPCS

46: The Dallas Morning News/KRT

49: Ben Liebenberg/NFL/SPCS

50: Michael Rooney/SPCS

55: Newsday/MCT

Front cover: Greg Fiume/Getty Images

Front cover inset: Chris McGrath/Getty Images